This book belongs to

- - - - - - - - - - - - - - - -

Books by Tom Percival published by
Macmillan Children's Books

Dream Defenders
Erika and the Anger Mare
Chanda and the Devious Doubt
Silas and the Marvellous Misfits

Little Legends
The Spell Thief
The Great Troll Rescue
The Genie's Curse
The Magic Looking Glass
The Secret Mountain
The Story Tree

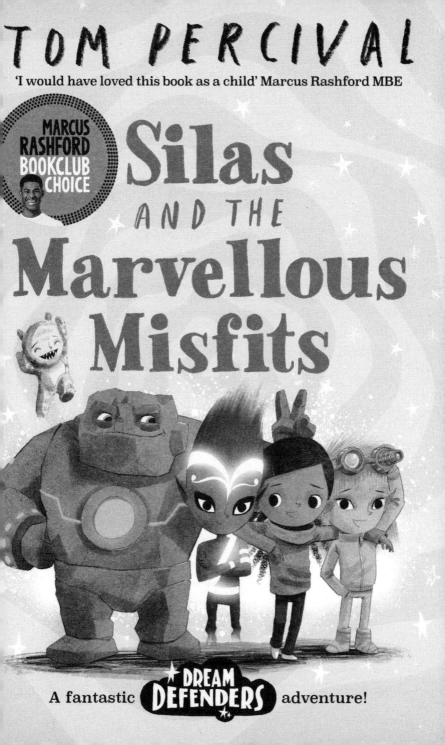

TOM PERCIVAL

'I would have loved this book as a child' Marcus Rashford MBE

MARCUS
RASHFORD
BOOKCLUB
CHOICE

Silas
AND THE
Marvellous
Misfits

A fantastic **DREAM DEFENDERS** adventure!

First published 2021 by Macmillan Children's Books
an imprint of Pan Macmillan
The Smithson, 6 Briset Street, London EC1M 5NR
EU representative: Macmillan Publishers Ireland Ltd, 1st Floor,
The Liffey Trust Centre, 117–126 Sheriff Street Upper
Dublin 1, D01 YC43
Associated companies throughout the world
www.panmacmillan.com

ISBN 978-1-5290-2919-2

1 3 5 7 9 8 6 4 2

A CIP catalogue record for this book is available from the British Library.

Printed and bound by CPI Group (UK) Ltd, Croydon CR0 4YY

With thanks to Holmen Paper, Gould Paper Sales
and CPI Books for their support.

This book is dedicated to the most wonderful and highly esteemed Salote Thacker.

I hope that you enjoy it, Salote!

Welcome to my Book Club.

I'm so excited that you are able to join us. I hope you have a smile on your face today.

*The book I have hand-selected for you is **Silas and the Marvellous Misfits**. It's a great story that shows you just how special it is to be yourself – to champion and celebrate the difference in one another.*

This book is for you to escape into, it's to inspire you and to help you to find adventure. And it belongs to you and only you – I want you to take it home tonight and write your name in it. Tell your friends that this book was chosen by me for you.

If you're struggling, don't be afraid to ask for help. We all need help along the way – me included. Enjoy every word at your own pace and remember that there's no rush to get to the end.

Get that head of yours high and let's conquer the day together.

With love,

MR

CHAPTER 1

Erika swam upwards through a cloud that smelled strongly of marshmallows. She glanced over at Beastling, swimming along beside her. He smiled and mumbled, **'Heebie Jeebie,'** through the thickening cloud.

As he spoke, a speech bubble popped out of his mouth, showing a picture of a thumbs up and a smiley face. Erika grinned and looked down at her timer. Twenty-five seconds. That was all they had before the cloud turned into a marshmallow and plunged to the ground in a deadly (but completely delicious) mess. This was not something that Erika wanted to happen – at least, not with them still inside the cloud!

BZZZZZT!

Erika's communications device buzzed and a gravelly voice spoke. 'Hey, Erika.

Listen, while you're back at Head Quarters getting that truth cannon, can you bring me a couple of doughnuts please?'

'What?' gasped Erika, struggling not to breathe in too much marshmallow. 'Look, Wade, I'm kind of busy right now!'

'Oh yeah, of course,' replied Wade. 'Sorry. And good luck!' There was a pause. 'But don't forget the doughnuts.' Then he ended the call.

Erika shook her head and swam faster.

Seventeen seconds later, Erika and Beastling popped out the top of the cloud, just as it became too thick to swim through. They sprinted to the edge and leaped off as the marshmallow cloud began to tumble towards the ground far below. Beastling followed close behind her. He *had* to. Erika and Beastling were bonded together, which meant that they could only ever be a few metres apart from each other. It had been that way since Erika's first adventure in the Dreamscape. Well, technically, it was ever since Beastling had first *bitten* her that they'd been bonded together – but that was a long time ago, and there was no point getting upset about it now.

Cold wind tore at Erika's skin as Beastling manoeuvred himself through the air and grabbed her shoulders. She thrust her arms and legs out in a star

shape and glowing sheets of
light spread between her hands
and feet like wings, creating a flying
suit that Erika could steer and control.

'Only the best for the **DREAM
DEFENDERS**, right?' yelled Erika, grinning.
If she tried to tell her friends at school

about any of this they would think she had gone mad! It wasn't like you could just say, 'By the way, I'm part of the **DREAM DEFENDERS**, a top-secret organization that helps children solve any problems they're having in their dreams.'

Her friends hadn't even believed her when she said her uncle had a Ferrari, so there was NO WAY they'd believe any of *this*!

To be fair to Erika's friends, her uncle *didn't* have a Ferrari. But he did have a red car that looked kind of sporty.

Erika twisted her body around, steering them towards the flattened top of an upside-down mountain in the distance. She looked at the impossible world around her as they shot through the air: far below a forest grew on the underside of a nearby cloud. The Dreamscape really was an amazing place.

A couple of seconds later they landed on the top of the mountain.

'**Heebie Jeebie!**' cried Beastling, punching the air excitedly. A speech bubble appeared with a picture of a female sheep and a cheese grater in it. Erika smiled and ruffled Beastling's fur.

'Ewe grate too!' she said with a grin. 'Let's get inside and find the others!'

Erika and Beastling crept down a roughly carved set of steps leading deep within the mountain. Damp, stale air drifted lazily down the corridor as Erika peered around.

'Where is everyone?' she muttered. 'This is where we were supposed to meet.'

'*Psst* . . . Erika!' a voice suddenly whispered from behind her.

Erika yelped and spun around – there was nobody there.

'Sorry!' continued the voice. 'I didn't mean to startle you. I know it can be dangerous for a human's heartbeat to become too elevated. Do you want me to hum some soothing music?' The disembodied voice stopped speaking and started humming. Badly.

'Silas?' interrupted Erika. 'Is that you? Why are you invisible? And *please* stop humming.'

The humming stopped. 'Oh. Am I still invisible?'

'*Yes!*' replied Erika.

'Ah! Right. Give me a second . . .' The air shimmered and suddenly the drifting, insubstantial figure of a boy appeared. Swirls of light covered his face and body, and even when he was fully visible he still faded away to nothing just below the knees.

'Ta-daaaa!'
exclaimed Silas.
'Better?'

'Much better!' said Erika.
'So, have you worked out how
to solve Miles's problem
yet?'

Silas shook his head. 'Not yet, but *hopefully* the truth cannon will help! Did you get it?'

Erika nodded and Beastling pointed to the weighty backpacks they were both carrying.

'Great!' exclaimed Silas. 'Wade and Sim have gone ahead to the centre of the mountain with Miles. That's where all the negative energy is coming from.'

'So, what are we waiting for?' asked Erika. 'Let's go!'

CHAPTER 2

Erika, Silas and Beastling were walking towards the centre of the mountain when a loud rumbling started. Erika glanced at Silas, who frowned, peering into the darkness.

A colossal CRASH echoed down the tunnel, followed by heavy, bone-shaking thuds that threw them off balance. Dust and grit fell from the ceiling.

'**Heebie Jeebie?**' asked Beastling, creating a question mark in the air.

'I don't know,' replied Erika. 'But it *doesn't* sound good . . .'

'I wonder if it might be prudent of us to hurry up,' suggested Silas. 'To increase our urgency? It's my belief that in these moments every second is vital, and we must make sure we don't waste any time—' He looked around and realized that Erika and Beastling were already sprinting ahead. 'Ah, yes. Well, that's what I was *trying* to say . . .' Then, using his super speed, he shot off, catching up with them in milliseconds.

Erika peered around the edge of a wall into the central chamber of the mountain. A full-scale battle raged between two giant robots and the other members of the **DREAM DEFENDERS**. As Erika watched, Wade used his powers to manipulate the rock of the mountain

into tall columns that rose up
from the floor. As he did this, a
giant lizard creature leaped from pillar
to pillar, flinging itself into the air and
turning into an eagle.

'Look,' cried Erika, pointing
at the eagle. 'There's Sim!'

The two massive robots were hurling
rocks, firing laser beams and trying to
stamp on Wade and Sim. Next to them

a third, smaller robot was motionless, its head drooping.

The eagle swept through the air, trying to rescue a struggling boy who was trapped in one of the giant, robotic hands – it was Miles, the child whose dream they were trying to fix. It looked as though the robots were trying to put him into the third, smaller robot.

'*Right!*' shouted Silas. 'You and Beastling get round behind them. Stay out of sight. When you've got a clear shot, use the truth cannon, then we'll finally know what all this is about! I'll go help Wade and Sim.' Then he was gone in a blur of light and shadow that left a trail behind, like a sweeping line painted on to the scene.

Darting from one hiding place to the next, Erika and Beastling sped around the edge of the chamber, looking for an opening to use the truth cannon.

All about them the battle raged. Wade built a huge stone prison around the robots – but they were too strong and easily demolished it. Sim was now in the shape of a lion with webbed dragon's wings. She did everything she could to get Miles out of the mechanical grasp of the creature, but whenever she got close the robots simply batted her away.

In no time, Miles was fixed into the smaller robot's head. As soon as he was encased within the huge metal structure, Miles's face fell, his expression slack and lifeless as his robot whirred into life.

The Miles robot swung a fist round, sending Wade crashing into a wall. One of the larger robots grabbed Sim, and with a grinding of gears and motors, the other rounded on Silas.

'*No!*' yelled Erika, pressing the ignition button on the truth cannon. A blistering jolt of light burst out, tearing through the air and slamming into the tallest robot. It jerked backwards with the force.

In the vivid beam of the cannon, Erika could see straight through the robot. Her mouth hung open. Inside, all the cables, wires and hardware which powered the robot looked like a face. A face she recognized—

Miles's mum!
Erika had seen
a picture of her in their
briefing earlier at **DREAM**
DEFENDERS HQ. She
quickly spun the cannon's
beam round to the other huge

robot. It revealed the face of Miles's dad.

But what did it mean?

Erika frowned and squinted up at the robots. It looked like they were operating Miles's robot with some kind of remote control.

'That's it!' she cried, tapping the communication device on her wrist. 'Miles feels like his family are too controlling. *That's* the problem! We need to work out how to make Miles feel like he can take control of his own life, so he can be who *he* wants to be.'

'What if we get the remote controller away from them, and give it to Miles?' asked Sim. 'Then he'll be able to control *himself*!'

The dazzling bolt from the truth cannon was wearing off, and the giant robots were grinding back into life.

'I'm on it!' yelled Wade, clambering out of the pile of gravel he'd made when he hit the wall. He ran as fast as he could towards the robots. This was surprisingly fast for a man made entirely out of stone, but even so it wasn't fast enough. The largest robot swung its leg round, kicking Wade right back into the same hole he'd just made in the cavern wall.

'Seriously?' groaned Wade's voice from beneath a pile of rubble.

The robot stomped over to where Wade was buried, but before it could do anything Sim swooped down and grabbed the controller in her powerful claws.

'*Yes!*' exclaimed Erika. 'Great work, Sim! Silas, can you go and help Wade?'

There was no response. Erika spun around.

Silas was standing completely still, staring up at the robots with an expression on his face that Erika had never seen before.

'Silas!' she shouted into her communication device. 'What are you doing?'

'*What?*' murmured Silas's indistinct voice.

'Move!' yelled Sim, as the robots turned their heads, their attentions, and all of their weapons, towards Silas. 'Get out of there, *NOW!*'

Silas blinked and appeared to wake up – but slowly, as though he was moving underwater. Sim dropped the controller and swooped down, picking Silas up just before a lethal death ray vaporized the rock where he had been standing.

Erika looked at the remote control.

The robots looked at the remote control. Erika looked at the robots.

'**Heebie Jeebie!**' yelped Beastling, making a picture of an Olympic sprinter, but Erika was already running.

On the other side of the cavern, the robots were running too. Huge pistons pumped and pounded as gears whirred and engines whined. They were far bigger, but Erika was more nimble.

With only seconds to spare, Erika leaped forwards and grabbed hold of the huge remote control. Using all her strength she was able to move the heavy levers, making the robot with Miles inside turn towards her. It towered over her as she made it reach out its huge metal hand to pick up the controller.

Once the Miles robot held the device in its own hands it paused, and inside the cockpit Miles blinked. He looked around in surprise and confusion. Tentatively, he moved the controls one way, and then the other, smiling as he realized that now *he* was in control.

With a decisive gesture, Miles made the robot drop the remote control on the floor and, glaring across at the two larger robots, stamped its foot down. The controller was crushed into pieces.

The two larger robots' heads immediately drooped down. All the thundering, clanking, whirring sounds, which had filled the chamber, fell away to nothing. For a moment, all Erika could hear was the heavy gasping of her own breath.

They'd done it!

Wade heaved himself out of the debris as Sim swooped down and placed Silas on the ground nearby. He looked down at the floor and scratched the back of his neck.

'Look – I'm . . . sorry,' he muttered softly. 'I messed up. I nearly ruined the whole mission.'

It was as though a light, which usually shone within him, had been turned off.

'But it was all fine in the end!' said Sim, patting him on the arm. 'We've totally sorted it!'

'No thanks to me,' said Silas quietly. 'Anyway, let's finish up and get back to HQ.'

'Yeah, good idea!' said Wade. 'Then we

can go and get some doughnuts, right?
Fancy that, Silas?'

Silas shook his head,

'Maybe not tonight . . .'

'Hey, Silas,' said
Erika, putting her
hand on her
friend's shoulder.
'Are you OK?'

A pang of alarm shot through her as Silas turned to face her. Everything about his expression was unfamiliar. He looked hollowed out and empty.

'I'm fine,' he muttered, without looking directly at her. 'Come on, let's get Miles out of that robot.'

'OK . . .' said Erika, watching as Silas walked away, shoulders sloping and defeated. It was hard to say exactly what was going on, but one thing was certain – Silas was most definitely *not* fine.

CHAPTER 3

The following morning Erika woke up in her bed, thinking hard.

They had fixed Miles's dream and got everything back on track. Mission accomplished. So why did her stomach still feel like she was on a rollercoaster?

It had *everything* do with Silas. He had just seemed so . . . wrong. So unlike Silas. Erika frowned as she got dressed. She was still thinking about her friend as she went downstairs for breakfast. Her parents were in the kitchen with

Randall, her younger brother, who was happily slopping mashed banana all over the table.

'Wicka!' he called out when he saw her. 'Wicka wake!'

'Hey, buddy!' she said, leaning over and tickling Randall's belly until he gurgled with delight.

'Morning, Erika,' called her mum

'Sleep all right?' added her dad. He peered at her and then continued, 'You look a bit tired. Everything OK?'

Erika paused for a moment. There was no way she could tell her parents about Silas. Firstly, the **DREAM DEFENDERS** were top secret, and secondly, whenever she told them something about one of her friends they *automatically* assumed she was talking about herself. They'd do the "Worried Parent Look" when they thought she wasn't watching and then have a whispered conversation about her later.

So, she tried her best to put her worries about Silas aside and smiled her biggest, brightest, most convincing smile.

'Yeah, I'm fine!' she said. 'Just could've done with another half hour's sleep I guess!'

'Tell me about it!' said her dad, grinning and giving Randall a pretend glare. '*Someone* woke me up at six thirty today!'

'Play-play!' chuckled Randall. 'FUN!'

'Yes ...' agreed Erika's dad uncertainly. '*Fun.*'

'Anyway, what do you fancy doing

today?' asked Erika's mum. 'I thought we could take a walk into town. Look in a few shops, get lunch from Cafe YUM. What do you think?'

Erika's eyes lit up, all thoughts of Silas momentarily driven from her mind. Cafe YUM was one of her all-time favourite places. They sold a HUGE selection of milkshakes, which had so many additional toppings that they stretched the definition of the word 'milkshake' to its very limits.

'YES!' she cried out immediately, wondering what she had done to deserve such a treat. A trip to Cafe YUM didn't usually just happen.

'We just need to do a few things first,' said her mum casually. 'I need some new stationery, your dad needs to go to the post office.' Then she added very quietly, almost under her breath, 'And you've got a trip to the dentist.'

Erika grimaced.

Why did parents always do this? You could never just do something nice for no reason.

'Oh, come on!' said her dad, smiling a bit too broadly. 'It'll be fun! You know, they give you those stickers, right?'

Erika snorted. 'Last time they gave

me a sticker saying "SMILE if you like healthy teeth!" I couldn't even feel my face, let alone smile.'

Her dad's smile stayed locked firmly in place. 'But that was after you'd fallen off your bike! This is just a check-up. We'll be in and out in minutes. Besides, you like your dentist don't you? She's nice.'

Erika glowered. Otters were *nice*. Kittens were *nice*. Sunny walks through the woods were *nice*. Dr McDrillem, the austere lady who barely said anything until Erika's mouth was wide open and filled with all sorts of dental tools, was *none* of those things.

'So . . . let's get this straight,' said Erika, her eyes narrowing. 'If I go to the dentist with no fuss, I can have *whatever*

I like at Cafe YUM?'

Her parents glanced at each other.

'I suppose . . .' said Erika's dad slowly.

'OK, it's a deal,' replied Erika briskly.
A triple scoop of ice cream with bubble-gum sauce and a flake on top of one of
Cafe YUM's signature SUPA-THIK-SHAKES was worth a trip to the dentist.

As it turned out, the appointment
at the dentist was
fine. Yes,

Dr McDrillem had waited until Erika's mouth was jammed open to ask whether she was working hard at school like a good little girl. And yes, she had made all her usual tutting noises as she peered judgementally into Erika's open mouth. But at least it hadn't taken *too* long.

And now Erika was sitting at her favourite table, in her favourite cafe, with her favourite milkshake, while her parents tried to keep Randall occupied. They were fighting a losing battle. The only game that Randall seemed to want to play was *Push the Ketchup Bottle off the Table*. He was very good at it too, much better than her parents were at playing *Catch the Falling Ketchup Bottle*.

'Shall we go now?' asked Erika's mum in a thin, brittle voice.

'Mum!' said Erika indicating her almost-full milkshake. 'I've not even got through the toppings yet!' Her mum's shoulders slumped.

'I'll take Randall to get something from the toy box,' said Erika. She held her hand out and helped Randall down from the table.

'Right!' she said as she led him over to the huge toy chest in the corner of the cafe. 'Let's find you something to play with.'

Randall murmured happily to himself as he fished through the toys, picking them up one by one. He settled on a doll in a long sparkling gown that Erika recognized.

'Hey!' she said happily. 'I've got one of these at home! I loved playing with her when I was your age! She sings a song when you pull this string.' Erika pulled the string, but no sound came out. 'Hmm, must be broken . . . Still, she's loads of fun!' As they walked back to the table, she demonstrated all the things that Princess Sparkleadore could do.

Randall played happily with the doll while Erika finished her milkshake. Her mum sat and read her book for a while, but her dad kept frowning and looking awkwardly over at Randall.

'Do you think Randall should be playing with a . . . well . . . *you know*?' he asked Erika's mum, nodding towards the doll in Randall's hands.

'What's that?' asked his wife, looking up from her book.

'Well, he's got a . . . *doll*.'

'Yeah,' replied Erika, 'an AWESOME doll!'

'Yes . . .' said Erika's dad, looking flustered. 'But still, shouldn't he have something a bit more . . . *you know* . . .'

'No,' said Erika's mum, looking confused. 'I don't *know*. Randall was bored, and now he's playing happily. What's the problem?'

'But it's a *doll*!' said Erika's dad loudly. 'I'll get him something more suitable.' He stood up and strode over to the toy chest, picking up a toy car and an action figure.

He then marched back and took Princess Sparkleadore out of Randall's hands.

Things rapidly went downhill from there.

Randall cried out in frustration. His little face crumpled at the interruption to his game and when the car was placed on the table in front of him, he bashed it furiously aside. It shot off the table and knocked over an old lady's cup of tea. The cup fell to the floor with a crash that startled one of the waitresses so much that she dropped her tray of SUPA-THIK-SHAKES all over an angry-looking man on the next table.

'Oh, for *goodness'* sake!' exclaimed Erika's mum, glaring at her husband. 'Now look what you've done!'

She apologized profusely to the old lady, the grumpy man

and the cafe owners, who all glared icily back at her, even when she offered to pay to cover the costs.

'I think we'd better leave,' whispered Erika. Her half-finished drink was still on the table as Randall, wailing like a siren, reached out his hands towards Princess Sparkleadore, who was lying discarded on the shiny plastic chair.

Erika's parents argued all the way home, and nothing seemed to cheer Randall up.

That evening, things went from bad to worse. Their food was burnt to a crisp when the timer didn't go off, so they had to cobble together an emergency dinner from one medium-sized potato, some wilted broccoli, a crust of not-quite-completely-stale bread and five and a half fish fingers. They ate the horrible meal in silence.

Then, to cap it all off, the boiler broke down, meaning Erika had to have a bath in about two inches of lukewarm water. But she *still* managed to accidentally drop her book into it, so its pages ended up as curled and messy as a bag of pencil shavings.

All in all, it was a relief when it was time for Erika to go to bed. At least now she'd be able to meet back up with the **DREAM DEFENDERS** and find out what was going on with Silas.

CHAPTER 4

It was a strange sensation, waking up into a dream, but Erika was used to it now. As soon as she fell asleep, she found herself standing by the circular dream portal that opened out from her dream into the wider world of the Dreamscape. Usually, Silas would meet her here and they would chat and laugh together as he led her up to the briefing room for that night's mission.

But not tonight.

Instead of Silas's smiling face, she was

confronted by Wade's granite features. He looked cross, which wasn't a surprise. Wade was usually cross about *something*. But there was another expression rippling across his face too. Was it worry? Concern? Sim and Beastling were standing there as well, both looking pale.

'What's going on?' she asked. 'Where's Silas?'

'It's a long story,' replied Sim, heading off at a quick walk. 'I'll tell you when we get there.'

'Get where?' asked Erika.

'**DREAM DEFENDERS** light pod station,' grunted Wade over his shoulder. '*Hurry up!*'

They strode briskly through the busy corridors of **DREAM DEFENDERS** HQ, following signs that led them towards the light pod station. Erika was almost running to keep up and Beastling was gasping behind her, their physical bond pulling him along with an almost magnetic force. Wade barged through the crowds and found a light pod big enough for the four of them. He marched over to it and glared at the junior **DREAM DEFENDERS** office worker who had just climbed in.

'I think you'll find this is *our* light pod,' growled Wade.

'Oh . . . is it? Silly me,' said the young man, scratching his antlers as he climbed nervously out. 'Sorry, Mr McRubble!'

'Mind it doesn't happen again,' muttered Wade.

'Sorry about that!' whispered Sim to

the trembling young man as they all climbed into the light pod.

The pods sat suspended on glowing beams of light that criss-crossed the station in a maddening, chaotic fashion.

'And these things never crash into each other?' asked Erika, as she watched a pod suddenly shoot off at a dizzying speed.

'Never,' replied Sim. 'Well, hardly ever anyway.' She pressed a button and a map appeared on the wall beside her. She squinted at it. 'I'd sit down and hold on to something though, if I were you.'

Erika grabbed a seat rest just as Sim called out, 'OK, pod, take us to Sector 7719!' and the light pod shot down the shimmering line at an immense speed.

'Is *anyone* going to tell me where

we're going?' demanded Erika.

'OK ...' sighed Wade. 'Basically, we have a problem. A *BIG* problem. Silas has gone missing!'

'Missing?' repeated Erika, horrified.

Wordlessly, Sim held out a sheet of paper. Erika took it and read aloud, her stomach churning.

I'm sorry for what happened in Miles's dream. I messed up. I froze and nearly ruined the whole mission. Just like I ruin everything.

You see, that dream made me think about my family, my people. I never felt like I fitted in at home. I didn't feel like I belonged. And in the end, I did what I always do, I ran away — I abandoned my family. So, now I need to fix things. I need to find a way to fit in.

I'm sorry — for everything.

Silas

Erika looked up. 'But . . .' she spluttered. 'I don't understand!'

'He returned *all* his **DREAM DEFENDERS** equipment,' said Sim, 'and even . . .' she paused, blinking quickly and wiping away a tear before finishing in a small, broken voice, 'his **DREAM DEFENDERS** pencil case.'

'He did WHAT?' exclaimed Erika. 'Silas LOVES that pencil case.'

'I know,' said Sim shaking her head.

'Right . . .' breathed Erika slowly, struggling to take in this avalanche of information.

'The *good* news,' added Sim, 'is that we know where he's gone.'

'Great!' cried Erika. 'So, that's where we're going now? To find him and talk him round? Problem solved, right?'

'Wrong,' rumbled Wade's gravelly monotone. 'Silas has gone *home*.' He gave Erika a meaningful look.

Erika blinked. 'What's so bad about that? Wouldn't most people go home when they feel upset or low?'

'Yeah,' growled Wade. 'But *most* people don't come from the Citadel of the Umbra, do they?'

Beastling murmured, '**Heebie Jeebie**,' and a speech bubble appeared, showing a cloud that was raining down even more dark clouds of rain.

'Everyone calls the Umbra the "**Glooms**",' explained Sim. 'And Beastling's right, they're *not* a lot of fun!'

'No,' muttered Wade. 'They enter human dreams and spread gloominess everywhere, making the dreamer feel sad, hopeless and dejected.'

'I can't tell you how many dreams they've messed up,' added Sim. 'And then *we* have to go in to fix them! Basically, the **Glooms** suck the joy out of your dreams and then use that energy to power their Citadel.'

Erika stared at Sim. 'But . . . that all sounds *so* unlike Silas!'

'Why do you think he left the Citadel in the first place?' replied Sim. 'It's not exactly like he fitted in there. I can't *believe* he's gone back!'

Erika took this information in as she stared out of the window. From her first Dreamscape adventure, Silas had been her best friend. A dull ache cut through her to think how awful he must be feeling to have run away like this.

She gritted her teeth. *She would get him back.* She would save him, the same way he'd saved her, countless times before.

Outside, the scenery became flatter, greyer. Any buildings they passed were shabby and dilapidated. As the landscape darkened around them, the pod began to rattle and vibrate as though the line of light it was travelling on was flickering and giving out.

'No one ever comes this far,' explained

Sim. 'The lines aren't maintained as well as they could be.' The vibrating grew worse, and a sharp, sour smell filled the air, as though rubber and plastic were being melted together.

Erika glanced back at Sim. 'Is something wrong with the pod?'

'It's not that,' replied Sim.

'Look outside.' Erika peered out as a dense, undulating mist rolled in.

'That's what you can smell,' added Wade. 'The **Glooms** *myst*. Nobody knows exactly what it is – it's what you might call . . . a *myst*-ery.' He paused and looked around expectantly. When no one said anything he shrugged. 'Well, *I* thought it was funny. Anyway, the whole Citadel is surrounded by this *myst* to keep people away. If you breathe it in then you start to give up on *everything* you ever believed in.'

'Sounds like they're not too keen on visitors,' said Erika.

Wade shook his head. 'In the past one hundred years there have been approximately zero people allowed into the **Glooms**' Citadel.' He paused. 'And in all that time only *one* person has ever come out.'

'**Heebie Jeebie?**' murmured Beastling, eyes wide.

'Yeah, who?' asked Erika.

Wade looked at them both for a

moment as if it should be obvious.

'Silas,' he replied in a grim voice.

CHAPTER 5

Shuddering and jolting, the pod ground to a halt just outside an abandoned light-line station.

'I guess we're here then,' said Erika, prising the door open and jumping out. As soon as she was in the thick tendrils of *myst*, the acrid, burning smell became even worse. She felt as though all colour had been drained from the world.

'This is hopeless,' she mumbled. 'Let's just turn back. We should give up and focus on something sensible. I might dedicate my life to a study of how many different grey things there are in the world.'

Beastling was muttering 'Heebie Jeebie' repeatedly and creating speech bubble after speech bubble filled with different grey colour swatches. Erika turned towards the pod and was about to clamber back in when Wade pulled out some breathing apparatus and helped fix it over Erika's head. Sim did the same for Beastling and for a moment they waited as Erika and Beastling took long, cool breaths of clean air.

'Feeling better now?' asked Sim.

Erika blinked, looking dazed and nodded slightly.

'Right. Let's get moving then,' said Wade.

Slowly, they walked through the dense, swirling *myst*, away from the station. Apart from the thin, flickering beam of light that had carried them here, there was no illumination in this flat, grey world.

After a while, Erika could make out a sheer, imposing cliff face, rising further than she could see. Carved into its wall was an ancient door surrounded by a foreboding gateway covered in strange runic symbols.

Erika peered up. It all looked so bleak and unfriendly. So *totally* the opposite of Silas.

She glanced over at Sim.

'What now?' she whispered.

Sim looked at Erika. 'I guess we knock?' she replied quietly.

Erika looked at Wade.

Wade shrugged and swung his heavy knuckles towards the door. There was a loud thud, but it was immediately swallowed up by the dense atmosphere – as though not even sound was welcome here. After a minute had passed, a grate slid open and a voice murmured, 'Go away.'

'Er, no – we can't do that. Sorry,' replied Sim. 'We're the **DREAM DEFENDERS** and we're looking for our friend.'

She held out her badge. There was silence as the grate slid shut. Then the door seemed to melt away, revealing a tall, shadowy figure. Like Silas, he had curling patterns of light swirling all over him and faded away below the knees, drifting gently, like smoke on the breeze. But his expression was completely different; cold and hard, as though he had never once laughed in his life. He was holding a number of jagged, unfriendly looking weapons, all with sharp, glowing tips.

'Oh? The Dream Police?' the guard said in a slow, monotonous voice. 'How nice of you to visit. However, as I'm sure you're aware, your rules do not apply here and you are not welcome.'

'We're not going anywhere until we've spoken with our friend!' shouted Wade.

'Gosh . . .' said the guard, not sounding shocked at all. 'Aren't *you* angry? Well, I'm afraid that your temper tantrum won't help you through our enchanted door.'

Wade lunged forwards and tried to barge past the shadowy figure, but suddenly stopped short. There was a reverberating crash and Wade was sent stumbling backwards, looking dazed.

'Oh dear . . .' said the guard, a smile on his thin lips. 'Which part of "*enchanted door*" did you not understand?'

Sim stepped forwards, putting her hand lightly on Wade's arm, steering him away, then she turned back to the guard.

'Look,' she said. 'I get it. We can't come in. That's fine. But can we just speak to our friend?'

'And who is this friend of yours?' asked the guard.

'You *know* who!' bellowed Wade spinning round to the door, but once again Sim steered him away.

'Our friend is called Silas Midlake,' said Erika. 'We know that he's here.'

'Oh?' said the Gloom, sounding bored. 'I see . . . well, the outcast you call "Silas" is no more. He has returned to his true home. He has re-sworn the Umbra oath.'

A sickly feeling rose through Erika. '*But* . . . that can't be right?'

'Indeed,' replied the guard. 'He has reclaimed his rightful, true Umbra name of Drythus Deadheart Midlake Melancholia.'

'*Seriously?*' asked Erika, raising an eyebrow. 'That's his *actual* name now?'

'Yes!' replied the guard, his eyes narrowing. 'Why? What's wrong with it?'

'Well,' said Erika, 'it's a bit over the top. He might as well be called Nohope Saddy Glum Sadface.'

The guard glared at her.

'My mother's name is Nohope. It is a fine and honourable Umbra name!'

'Look,' said Sim, rushing over and steering Erika out of the way too. 'I feel like we're all getting off on the wrong foot here. Let's just start again, shall we?'

'A marvellous idea,' said the guard as the doorway magically reappeared. 'And I believe the first thing I said to you was . . . *GO AWAY*!' Then the grate on the door slid shut, leaving Erika, Wade, Sim and Beastling alone in the bitter, drifting *myst*.

'So, what *now*?' asked Erika, tears of frustration pricking at her eyes. 'Silas is in there. He'd never leave any of us behind! We've GOT to get inside.'

'And we will!' said Sim, patting Erika's arm. 'We *will* get him back!'

'But how?' pushed Erika. 'There's no other way in, just a huge, stone cliff face.'

'**Heebie Jeebie** . . .' said Beastling slowly,

looking at
Erika and
making
a picture
of Wade
tunnelling
through a
giant rock.

'Oh yeah!' said Erika. 'I forgot about that!'

'Typical!' muttered Wade. 'Whenever people think about superpowers it's always *flying-this* or *super-strength-that*. Nobody ever recognizes my craft!'

'Come on then,' said Sim. 'Let's put Wade's amazing abilities to good use!'

'Are you being sarcastic?' grunted Wade, glaring at Sim.

Sim sighed. 'No, Wade. Gosh, you're *so* sensitive!'

'Well, it *sounded* sarcastic,' replied Wade.

'Heebie Jeebie!' said Beastling, making a speech bubble with a sand timer running out.

'For once I agree with the furball!' said Wade. 'Come on, let's *do* this!'

CHAPTER 6

Silently, Wade created a tunnel that led through the cliff face, deep underground towards the **Glooms**' Citadel.

'This map looks pretty old,' said Erika holding up a piece of ancient, musty-smelling parchment which Sim had brought from **DREAM DEFENDERS** HQ. 'Are you sure it's up to date?'

'Not really,' said Sim. 'But it's the best we've got!'

The map was titled *Ye Olde Umbra Citadel* and showed a scratchy drawing of a huge, spiralling structure, burrowing deep beneath the ground. It was surrounded by various traps and pitfalls with names like **SOUL-CRUSH BOULDER-SLIDE**, **EVISCERATION ALLEY** and **CAVERN OF THE STUBBED TOES.**

Ye Olde Umbra Citadel

Doo

Sou
Co
Bou
Sl

Evisc
A

Cavern
Stub

'Heebie Jeebie!' muttered Beastling, creating a picture of a toe hitting a table leg, an equals sign and then a series of squiggly symbols.

'*Beastling!*' exclaimed Erika. 'Mind your language!'

'*Shhh!*' whispered Wade, his hands pressed to the granite in front of them. 'We're nearly there! I can feel vibrations.'

'Great!' replied Sim. 'If you open up a small hole we can check if we're clear to carry on.'

'Will do,' muttered Wade. He frowned with concentration, pushing all his focus through his outstretched hands and deep into the mountain.

Erika gasped. She was used to seeing Wade tunnelling through rock, but it was usually a messy, chaotic process. In slow motion, it was as though the stone somehow turned to liquid and flowed wherever Wade wanted it to go. Ever so slowly, the rock smudged round, like a whirlpool that led down to a hole about a centimetre wide.

Erika leaned forward to peer through. She yelped and leaped backwards.

'*What?*' hissed Wade. 'What's wrong?' He leaned forwards and gasped. Peering back at him from the other side of the hole was another eye.

An Umbra eye.

'*OK . . .*' he said. 'So, we don't go *that* way! Let's go back up the tunnel to the—'

'Stay where you are!' instructed a familiar-sounding voice from behind them. 'You're completely trapped!'

'*Silas?*' asked Erika, spinning around. 'What's going on?'

But it wasn't Silas. It was someone who looked and sounded a *lot* like him.

'I'm not *Drythus*,' said the Gloom who was blocking their path. 'I'm his sister, Despondia. But I *will* tell you what's going on. You are now my prisoners.'

'But . . . how did you find us?' asked Sim.

Despondia blinked at her. 'The next time you intend to break into a highly secure location, I would advise you not to discuss your plan right outside that highly secure location's gateway!' Despondia smiled ever so slightly. 'Not that there will be a next time. Now . . .

you will do everything that I say. Or you will *die*. Is that clear?'

She clicked her fingers and a squadron of Gloom soldiers ran into the tunnel behind her, weapons at the ready.

The **DREAM DEFENDERS** leaped into action. Sim was morphing into a Tyrannosaurus rex as Wade stretched out his hands to open the stone floor beneath the **Glooms** into a huge pit. But before

they could do anything, Despondia clicked her fingers again.

'Wrong answer,' said the Gloom girl.

Sim was half transformed into a dinosaur and looking around in confusion. 'I'm stuck!' she half spoke, half roared. Wade frantically thrust out his hand towards the stone, but nothing happened. Their powers were gone.

'I'm sure your tricks are impressive elsewhere in the Dreamscape,' said Despondia, 'but down here, in *our* world, they are meaningless. Now let's try again, shall we? You will do everything that I say –' she smiled a thin, humourless smile – 'or, as I *believe* I have already mentioned . . . you will die.'

CHAPTER 7

Drifting manacles of shadow were bound tightly around Erika's wrists. She wriggled and twisted her hands, but couldn't get them free. Erika, Beastling, Wade and Sim were led down the musty passageways, spiralling deep into the Citadel, further underground. Tonnes of rock pressed in at Erika from all angles.

'Impressive, isn't it?' asked Despondia. 'What you can feel is the weight of tradition. Thousands of years of Umbra heritage, all contained within our Citadel, all feeding into each and every one of us. Exactly as it is. Exactly as it always has been. That is the way of the Umbra.'

'That is the Umbra way!' chanted all the soldiers automatically.

'Creepy!' whispered Erika.

'What?' asked Despondia, her eyes narrowing.

'Can you even hear yourself?' asked Erika. 'Nothing stays the same forever!'

'The Umbra do!'

retorted Despondia. '*That* is the Umbra way.'

'*That is the Umbra way!*' echoed the soldiers in a chant.

'*No!* You weren't meant to do it *then*!' said Despondia glaring at the soldiers. 'I was just talking to the prisoner!' She shook her head and turned back to Erika. 'Do you know what we do with any voices that disagree with us?'

'I don't, but I'm fairly sure you're going to tell me . . .' said Erika.

'We silence them!' announced Despondia grandly, clicking her fingers. Erika tried to speak, but no sound came out. Her eyes shot wide open and she spun around to look at her friends. Their frustrated expressions made it clear that none of them could speak either.

'That's better,' said Despondia. 'Now prepare yourselves. You have an audience with . . . *the Forefather*!'

Erika mumbled and waved her manacled hands.

'What?' asked Despondia, frowning.

Erika gestured frantically, shrugging and waggling her eyebrows.

'I'm sorry, I have no idea what you mean. Can you draw the word with your hand?'

It was hard to do with her hands bound, but eventually Erika was able to trace a word in the air.

WHO?

'*Ahhh!*' replied Despondia. 'The Forefather is our leader. He is the living embodiment of *every* Umbra leader who has ever traipsed along these dusty hallways. From Gloomerius the Bleak, to Melancholia the Magnificent! Even Grumble the Slightly-Ticked-Off lives on in the Forefather, although no one really talks much about Grumble, he wasn't a great ruler to be honest.' She shook her head and continued, 'You see, all our leaders live on in the Forefather. It is with their combined wisdom and power that he will bring about his most ambitious plan yet, to unify the Dreamscape in one whole, wonderful world of UMBRA!'

'*That is the Umbra way?*' chanted the soldiers uncertainly.

'That was *perfect!*' said Despondia, nodding encouragingly. 'Well done!'

Erika and her friends were led out through a stone archway into a massive circular chamber. It was clearly the heart of the **Glooms**' Citadel. Row upon row of tiered seating lined the sloping floor. Every surface of the walls and ceiling were covered with hundreds of thousands of mirrors, all reflecting a slick, obsidian darkness.

As she walked, Erika gazed around the hall in awe. It was impressive – cold, austere and intimidating, but undeniably impressive. Most of the seats were occupied by

Glooms who were all facing towards the empty space in the centre of the hall, where thick threads of light spun and twisted lazily, like a slow-motion whirlpool in mid-air.

'Behold!' cried Despondia as Erika, Wade, Sim and Beastling were brought to a halt in front of the dancing lights. 'The ancient power vortex of the Umbra. This is what powers our whole Citadel, where all Umbra are born and where we all return to at the end of our time. Is it not impressive? Does it not strike awe into your frail human heart?' She glanced over at Erika expectantly.

Erika gestured to her closed mouth. Despondia sighed and clicked her fingers so Erika could talk again.

'Seriously?' said Erika, one eyebrow raised. 'Did you actually just say "*Behold*"? I have literally never heard anyone, *ever* say that word out loud.'

Despondia glared. 'It won't be long

before you, and *everyone* else, thinks and feels the same way as me. Your, *oh-so-funny* jokes won't amuse you then. In fact, nothing will amuse you, for what use do the Umbra have for amusement?'

'What do you mean?' asked Erika, looking at Despondia with narrowed eyes. Before Despondia could reply, a deafening, ominous sound filled the chamber. It was so thick with dread and foreboding that Erika felt as though she could almost reach out and touch it. It rose up through her, like nausea.

'The Forefather!' whispered Despondia. 'He approaches!'

Erika peered down in the same direction as Silas's sister, towards an archway covered with glowing symbols.

A light flared within the arch and a figure materialized. He stood taller than any of the other **Glooms** and, as he appeared in the room, the temperature seemed to drop. Every single Gloom in the chamber fell to their knees as the Forefather strode out into the centre of the hall and turned slowly around to face the assembled crowd.

He held up an ancient, leather-bound book, took a deep breath and said, 'We are the Umbra. We act and think as one.' His voice was hard and clear as it rang around the huge space.

'*That is the Umbra way!*' chanted the crowd in a dull monotone.

'My family!' called out the Forefather. 'Today is a momentous day. Our child,

Drythus, is returned to us. There was a low murmuring in the hall as light flared in the archway again. The Forefather held the book out once more as Silas stepped into the hall. Wade, Sim and Beastling's eyes all widened at the sight of their friend.

'Silas!' cried Erika, but nobody paid her any attention. Not even Silas.

She watched open-mouthed as he stepped out to stand by the Forefather's side.

It was as though someone else had taken over Silas's body. He stood there, cold and emotionless, his expression unreadable. Even though he was directly facing Erika, he gave no impression of having seen her at all.

Erika's heart sank. Perhaps this mission wasn't going to be *quite* as easy as she had thought.

CHAPTER 8

'Our numbers have increased by one,' proclaimed the Forefather. 'But soon, the ranks of the Umbra will swell by more. Many, *many* more!'

Erika frowned as he continued to speak.

'You have been working diligently, harvesting energy from the humans' dreams, and now our power vortex is stronger than ever before. You have performed your duties as true Umbra. With great levels of melancholy. Soon, very soon, we will save the Dreamscape.'

The crowd stood with bowed heads and chanted in unison, '*That is the Umbra way.*'

'We will help them see the shadow!' shouted the Forefather. 'They shall know the one true way. Very soon, we shall use the power held within our vortex to convert *everyone* to UMBRA!'

The crowd rose slowly to their feet chanting, '*Umbra! Umbra! Umbra!*'

'What?' gasped Erika. 'What's he on about?'

'*Shhhh!*' hissed Despondia.

Wade was led out in front of the power vortex, wrists tightly bound by the swirling shadow manacles that sapped him of all his strength and powers.

'I shall now read the ancient words, as described in the sacred text,' said the Forefather. 'And soon, our poor friend here will be saved! Reborn! As an *Umbra*!'

Wade's eyes widened, but he was unable to fight against the enchantments. Against his will, his feet moved towards the vortex, which opened like a mouth around him.

'No!' screamed Erika.

The Forefather's eyes misted over as he read from the book in a strange sibilant language. As he spoke, all the Umbra's eyes became blank and unseeing. Droning chanting echoed around the hallway as sharp gusts of wind spun and danced out of the vortex. Momentarily, the swirling lights flared to a dazzling brilliance and the air was filled with the smell of rain on hot tarmac. Then the light fell away almost to nothing.

Erika gasped as a figure stepped out. In many ways, it looked like Wade – large, strong and thickset, but also shadowy and insubstantial, covered with swirling patterns of light. The face showed no emotion whatsoever.

'And again, our numbers grow!' cried the Forefather, his eyes still a terrifying blankness. 'The Umbra way continues. Exactly as it is. Exactly as it always has been!'

'*That is the Umbra way!*' intoned the imitation of Wade in a flat, dull monotone.

'*Wade!*' screamed Erika, wrestling with her restraints. Sim turned to look at Erika. For a second their terrified eyes met, then Beastling was led out towards the gaping mouth of the vortex in front of them.

Erika felt the familiar tug that she always felt whenever Beastling moved more than a few metres away from her. He was at the very limit that they could comfortably be apart. The sharp pain tugged at Erika's side as Beastling's small body stepped jerkily towards the vortex.

It felt as though a coarse wire connected them. With every step that Beastling took, the wire tightened around Erika, with burning intensity. He stared desperately at Erika, but neither of them could do anything to stop what was happening.

'It's OK!' yelled Erika. 'Don't worry, Beastling, it'll all be OK. You'll see!'

Then Beastling's tiny body stepped fully into the vortex and vanished.

The ritual chanting built up to a crescendo again, just as it had when Wade entered the vortex. Again, Silas stood there, just like all the other Umbra, blank-eyed, blank-faced and chanting.

'Silas!' screamed Erika. 'You *have* to help! *Please!* You don't belong here. Don't you see? This is NOT *you*!'

He gave no indication that he had heard her at all.

The vortex swirled like a flock of birds swooping through a flaming sky. The ominous chants echoed around the chamber. They started to glitch and stutter, drifting out of tune with each other, until it all became a deafening cacophony.

Erika looked at the Forefather. He was still chanting, but seemed distracted, trying to see what was creating the disturbance. The swirling mass of energy twitched and convulsed like a wounded animal. Erika gasped as a powerful jolt coursed through her. The air was filled with energy and thrummed in her ears. She stumbled to one side as a violent tearing sound ripped through the chamber. Sparks and flames burst out of the vortex and all the lights in the room flickered. Then out stepped Beastling – still small, still furry, but made out of shadows and covered in swirling light patterns.

Erika sobbed as she looked at her little friend. She felt an ache inside her, which wasn't just sorrow.

They were no longer connected.

Erika didn't even notice as emergency alarms rang out in the chamber. Around her, the room was in uproar as waves of energy radiated from the vortex. Despondia's eyes returned to normal as she leaped forward to put out a fire that danced among a row of seats. Erika just stood there. Dazed. Vacant. A hand grabbed her arm and a voice hissed in her ear, 'Quickly! Erika! The power's down and our restraints are off. We need to go. Now!'

She felt as though she was deep underwater. The words drifted down to her, muffled and indistinct.

'*What?*' she murmured.

'Just follow me!' commanded Sim, grabbing Erika's arm. With clumsy, faltering steps, Erika was dragged away from the huge hallway and the hollow, empty shells that used to be Wade and Beastling.

CHAPTER 9

Erika sat within a small, hidden room. Sim had shape-shifted to look like a brick wall and was covering the doorway. From the outside, in the dim, gloomy light of the Citadel, nobody would know there was a room there.

Cold, hard stone pressed up against Erika's back. It was uncomfortable, but she barely felt it. She hugged her knees, staring blankly at the floor through tears that distorted her vision.

'There was nothing we could do,' said

Sim, for what felt like the twentieth time. 'That was our only chance to escape. And if we aren't free then how can we hope to rescue the others?'

'I know . . .' said Erika slowly. 'It just feels . . . weird. You know, every time I've come here – to the Dreamscape – I've had that connection with Beastling.

And now? It's *gone*. Does it mean that he's—' Her face crumpled and she started crying again.

'Shhhhh.' Sim tried to comfort Erika, but there wasn't much she could do as a wall. 'Look, I don't know exactly what any of this means. But I promise you – we are going to do everything we can to get our friends back. We just need a plan. We need to focus now. OK?'

'But what about Silas?' demanded Erika. 'He just stood there. He let this happen. How *could* he?'

'I don't know,' said Sim. 'But did you notice when the Forefather read from that book, their eyes all went blank? What do you think that means?'

'I don't care!' spat Erika angrily. 'He's

ruined everything. This is *all* Silas's fault!'

'Hey, come on, Erika. *Please* try to calm down,' said Sim. 'We don't want any **Glooms** to find us.'

Erika took a deep breath. She fought back at the anger that threatened to consume her.

What had happened, had happened. Being angry about it wasn't going to help. Sim was right. What they needed to do now was focus.

'You're right,' said Erika, looking over at Sim.

The two friends smiled at each other, then Erika continued, 'So, what are we going to do?'

'Well, first things first, we need to get out of this room,' said Sim. 'We can't just hide in here forever and besides, it's really boring being a brick wall! We can't do this alone, so we need to head back to HQ, get reinforcements and come back to rescue Wade and Beastling.' She paused for a moment. 'Silas too. If he *wants* to be rescued . . .'

It was easier said than done. The whole Citadel looked largely the same wherever they were – an endless maze of long, curling corridors filled with identical doors that led into other long, curling corridors filled with *equally* identical doors. As neither Erika nor Sim could understand the **Glooms**' language, the signs on the doors were not a lot of help. They could have said 'EXIT THIS WAY' or they might just as easily have said 'BURNING-HOT FIRE DEATH AWAITS ALL WHO ENTER'.

It didn't help that they had to keep hiding themselves away whenever someone walked past.

'That was a close one!' whispered Erika as she climbed out of a huge, sombre-looking urn.

'You're telling *me*!' replied the urn as it changed back into Sim.

Carefully, Erika prised a door open a couple of centimetres. When nothing terrible happened, she opened it wider and together they stepped through into yet another long passageway.

A cold, musty draft billowed down the corridor, sending a wave of dust rippling towards them.

'This place gives me the creeps!' muttered Erika, '*Why* would Silas have wanted to come back here?'

Sim shrugged. 'I guess because they're his family?' she said. 'I mean, it's tricky isn't it? He *wants* to belong. He *wants* to fit in. But the Silas we know is so far from all this . . . He must just be pretending so he can fit in.'

'Right . . .' said Erika slowly. 'It's not turned out very well so far, has it?'

'No,' agreed Sim. 'Not so far. At the end of the day, you've got to be true to yourself. You can't just keep changing to fit in with whoever happens to be around.'

Erika glanced over at Sim.

'Says the person who *literally* transformed into a unicorn the other night, just to get into a "Unicorns Only" theme park.'

'That's different!' protested Sim. 'I was just *pretending* to be a unicorn. Besides, those rides were awesome. And who wouldn't want to be a unicorn?'

'Fair enough,' said Erika grinning. They walked on in silence, their footsteps making no sound on the cushioning layers of dust.

'So, how about we—'

'*Run!*' interrupted Sim, her voice shrill and quavering.

'What?' asked Erika, looking up. Sim's face was pale, her eyes wide and staring over Erika's shoulder.

One of the doors ahead was swinging

open. A gleaming, sharp-edged weapon jutted from the door as the drifting, shadowy legs of a Gloom marched out.

CHAPTER 10

Erika gasped as the Gloom soldier stepped out through the door.

'Silas!' she whispered.

Silas stopped and regarded them. 'I am Drythus,' he said solemnly. 'And you must come with me.' He ushered them through the door he'd just walked out of.

Rows of ceramic buttons lined the carved wooden walls of the small room, alongside a huge plan of the entire Citadel.

'Is this some sort of...
elevator?' asked Sim.

'In a manner of
speaking,' replied Silas.
'Why?'

'Because you can move at the speed of light,' said Sim. '*And* teleport. Why do you need an elevator?'

'Those abilities are not to be used in the Citadel,' said Silas. 'Moving slowly and deliberately keeps us pure.'

'You even *sound* like a Gloom!' muttered Erika.

'What's going on, Silas?' asked Sim. 'How could you abandon us like that? You saw what happened to Wade and Beastling!'

Hot tears prickled at Erika's eyes. 'You've betrayed us!'

'As I say, my name is Drythus,' said the Gloom boy in front of them. 'And your friends will be better off now. They no longer have to worry about such meaningless distractions as happiness or fun.'

'But that's *insane!*' burst out Erika. 'You are literally the happiest person I've ever met! You can't pretend that you're not, just to try to fit in here!'

'I'm not *pretending* anything,' said Silas. 'I am an Umbra. And the Umbra way must continue—'

'Yeah, yeah, yeah, I know – exactly as it is. Exactly as it always has been,' interrupted Erika. 'You're like a completely different person. This isn't you!'

'Maybe it's more that the person you thought you knew wasn't me,' said Silas.

'You're driving me mad!' shouted Erika. 'Talking in riddles like that! Besides, this isn't just about you, it's about *everyone*.'

'You know the Forefather's plan,' added Sim. 'They're going to spread *myst* through the whole Dreamscape and convert *everyone* to Umbra! You can't want that to happen!'

A flicker of emotion shot across Silas's face. For a second, Erika felt as though she could see her friend again. Then the moment passed.

'I *am* an Umbra,' said Silas. 'And if *that* is the Umbra way, then so be it.'

'Yes. You *are* an Umbra!' replied Erika earnestly. 'But there's more to you than that! You're *Silas*. You're a member of the **DREAM DEFENDERS** . . .' Tears filled her eyes. 'You're my *friend*!'

Once again, there was the briefest flash

of the Silas that Erika knew, rippling across the face of this stranger. He made a gasping sound and a pained expression shot across his face.

'QUICKLY!' hissed Silas in his usual voice. 'You have to help! The Forefather is planning to turn everyone in the Dreamscape into an Umbra TONIGHT. There's no time!' He keyed in a code on the elevator buttons and the plan of the Citadel lit up. All the swirling Umbra script was replaced with writing that Erika could understand.

'It's *the book*! It's controlling us a—' He gasped in pain. 'Now go!'

'But Silas—' began Erika.

'Just *GO!*' gasped Silas, tears running down his face. 'I can't fight it for long . . .' Then he turned away from his friends and ran out of the elevator, the door sliding shut behind him with a cold, hard hiss.

CHAPTER 11

'What now?' asked Sim frantically.

Erika shook her head, her heart beating fast. 'We don't have time to go back to HQ any more! The Forefather is going to take over the whole Dreamscape. *Tonight!*'

'You're right,' agreed Sim. 'It looks like we're on our own . . . so what did Silas mean by "*the book*"?'

Erika frowned. 'Did you see that creepy old book the Forefather was holding?'

Sim's eyes widened. 'Yes! I'll bet it's

something to do with that!'

'And where would you keep a creepy old book?' asked Erika. 'Or *any* book really?'

'In a . . . library?' said Sim hesitantly.

'Yep!' exclaimed Erika. 'And now we know how to find it.'

She peered at the map on the wall. 'Right about . . . *there*!' She jabbed her finger at the room labelled 'Library' and Sim keyed in the code. A queasy, lurching sensation rose up in Erika's stomach as the elevator sped away. It turned and swung in all sorts of directions, sending Erika and Sim hurtling around the small room. An automated voice said, 'Remember. Always fully secure yourself before choosing your destination.'

'*Now*
they tell us!'
gasped Sim as
she bounced
off the ceiling
and rolled
along a wall.
Eventually
the elevator
slowed down
and they
both fell in
a heap on the
floor.

Erika sat
up groggily.
'Let's take

the stairs next time . . .' she muttered, then pressed the button to exit, and the doors silently slid open.

Row upon row of ancient books lined the walls of the huge room in front of them, towering from floor to ceiling. Dotted on uncomfortable-looking seats around the library were various **Glooms**, reading solemnly.

'*Ready?*' whispered Sim. Erika nodded and together they crept into the dusty corridors of heavy old bookshelves, which towered up everywhere. It was like being in a dizzying maze made of books.

Erika inspected a few of the spines and read *Happiness is Overrated, You Never Fail If You Never Even Try* and *I QUIT! 12 Simple Ways To Just Stop Bothering.*

She glanced over at Sim and shook her head.

For what felt like hours, they crept around the massive library, taking great care to avoid any **Glooms** that they saw. At one point, Erika was certain they had been spotted when they accidentally walked right out in front of an old Umbra man. Luckily, he had been far too absorbed in his book, *How To Be More Observant*, to notice them.

'How will we *ever* find the book we're looking for?' groaned Erika eventually.

Sim looked at her thoughtfully. 'What we need,' she said slowly, 'is a librarian.' She suddenly gasped. 'I have something that might help!' Sim excitedly pulled out her communication device and tapped a few buttons on it.

A hologram of a librarian appeared in the air in front of them.

'Hello, Sim!'

called the librarian in a loud voice. Erika leaped forwards and turned the volume down, until the librarian's voice was barely audible.

'So, what kind of book are we looking for today?' asked the librarian.

'I'm actually looking for something specific,' said Sim.

'Go on . . .' said the librarian.

'But I don't know the name of the author.'

'Mmmmm–hmmmm,' muttered the librarian, frowning slightly.

'*Or* the exact title of the book,' admitted Sim.

The librarian's shoulders slumped. 'OK. Do you know what it looks like?'

'Right. So, it's *mega*-old,' said Sim, 'with

swirly, glowing symbols on the front which I guess would be the title. And the pages look like they *might* have been made out of crushed hopes and dreams. I *do* know that it contains all of the Umbra's sacred texts.'

The librarian gasped. 'You don't mean . . . the *Umbra Book of Sacred Texts*?'

'Oh. So that's the title?' said Erika. 'Makes sense I guess . . .'

'Where is it?' asked Sim urgently.

'Why, in the reference section, of course!' replied the librarian. 'But I'll warn you now, it is a highly dangerous book. Are you sure you don't want something nicer?' She held up a book with two toy animals eating sandwiches. 'What about *Binky and Fluffkins Have a Lovely Picnic*?'

'No thanks,' said Erika. 'We really do need the *Umbra Book of Sacred Texts*.'

'*OK . . .*' muttered the librarian. 'But don't say I didn't warn you. The reference section is just over here.'

She turned and pointed towards a small door in the darkest, most distant corner of the library. It was locked, barred, chained and bolted.

'But I am NOT going in there with you!' said the librarian. 'Good day!' And she turned off her own projection before Erika or Sim could say anything else.

'How will we get in *there*?' groaned Erika.

Sim grinned and morphed into a giant set of keys.

'Great work, Sim!' whispered Erika, picking up the keys and getting silently to work. Soon, everything was unlocked and the heavy wooden door swung open.

CHAPTER 12

Swirling fog clung to the ancient flagstones and drifted through the dimly lit reference section. Carved stone pedestals rose up with ancient books resting on them. In the centre of the room was a dancing, glowing force field, flickering and buzzing. As Erika stepped closer, she felt her teeth vibrate. Within the force field was a stone plinth and, sat upon that, was the *Umbra Book of Sacred Texts*.

'How do we *get* to it?' whispered Erika.

'You *don't!*' boomed a voice. The Forefather materialized in front of them. He waved his hand and the gates behind them slammed shut.

'Hey!' exclaimed Sim. 'I didn't think you were allowed to teleport in here!'

For a second the Forefather paused, looking a bit awkward, then he continued,

'Sometimes these things have to be done! You've led us all in a merry dance, but now it's over.' He strode towards the force field and thrust his arm inside, pulling out the book. A violent, crackling buzz echoed around the library and the temperature dropped, as though the ancient volume was sucking all the life out of the room.

'You're too late,' said the Forefather, flicking through the book and stopping on a page filled with complex diagrams, showing lots of planets and stars.

'You see,' he said, 'on today's date, all

the planets, stars,
moons and asteroids in
the Dreamscape are perfectly aligned!
Now is the time to put our plan into action.
We can save the whole Dreamscape from
worrying about being fulfilled, or happy.
We can give them *all* the gift of Gloom!
The same conditions won't be repeated
for another . . .' he paused and did some
calculations on his fingers, 'thirty-two
thousand and sixty-seven years. And I
don't feel like waiting that long to save
the world.'

'Save the world? You're going to *end*
the world!' protested Erika. 'You're going
to make everyone just like *you*. Joyless,
cold and living by ancient rituals that
are complete nonsense!' She jabbed her

finger at a picture on the next page, showing a Gloom child with a duck sitting on top of its head. 'I mean, what is *that*?'

'How DARE you!' bellowed the Forefather. 'That is the ancient rite of Duck-Head-Time-Flow. On the third Wednesday of the first month of every other decade, the second youngest Umbra in each household must wear a duck on their head to prevent time from going backwards. If we were to NOT perform that ceremony, then time would reverse! Everyone would just get younger and younger, until they ceased to exist!'

'Except that *wouldn't* happen!' said Erika. 'How could putting a duck on your head stop time going backwards. It doesn't make sense!'

'It doesn't NEED to make sense!' shouted the Forefather. '*The book tells us it is so!*'

'But that's the problem!' insisted Erika. 'It's not *you* making these decisions, it's the book! That book is controlling *all* of you!'

The Forefather paused for a moment and looked closely at Erika, but then the book trembled in his hands. It sent vibrations up his arms in waves of energy and once again his eyes misted over.

'Silence!' he roared. 'You've wasted enough time. The planets are *all* in alignment. We must return to the vortex to start proceedings.'

He clicked his fingers and the door swung open. In marched a squadron of Gloom guards, led by the ghoulish figures of Wade and Beastling, silently carrying weapons, handcuffs and restraints.

'No!' yelled Erika. 'Wade! Beastling! *Stop!*'

But it was no good. Within seconds, both Sim and Erika were bound by shadows and led out of the room.

Erika was standing so close to the vortex that she could feel the energy thrumming out. Immense vibrations tore through the air at an incredible frequency. As the Forefather read from the book, all the Glooms' eyes clouded over – blank, white and unseeing. Soon, soldiers came and grabbed Erika and Sim, leading them towards the vortex.

Erika dug her heels in, she kicked, she struggled. As the Forefather read the incantation that would put her under the ancient book's control, she did

everything she could to ignore it. She repeated the words of her favourite story from when she was younger. She hummed the tune from an advert for toothpaste. Even as she felt she was losing control over her own body, Erika did everything she could to ignore the words.

The Forefather scowled.

'We don't have time for this,' he snapped. 'Leave them. We must activate the mirrors *now*.'

The guards nodded and turned away.

Erika slumped, her body heavy and unresponsive. Whatever the Forefather had been trying to do hadn't *fully* worked, but she definitely didn't feel right. Her mouth was drooping and leaden, as though it didn't belong to her at all. She glanced over at Sim, whose head was slumped down, eyes shut.

'*Sim* ...' she hissed desperately, but there was no response – the Forefather's magic had knocked her unconscious.

The Forefather's fingers twirled and spun around as he read. As the vortex behind him continued to grow, one by one, the mirrors in the hall flared into life.

'First, we harvest the last of the energy we need!' cried the Forefather in a loud, clear voice.

'And when the vortex is fully powered, the time of Umbra will be upon us! Ensuring the Umbra way continues. Forever, and always!'

'*That is the Umbra way!*' chanted the crowd.

Clouds swirled within the mirrors as indistinct images appeared. Erika gasped. Inside each mirror she could see a child – a human child.

She had never seen so many different faces in one place. Each child was asleep and clearly dreaming, oblivious to what was happening in the hall.

Erika tried to shout out, to scream, to stop whatever was about to happen, but all she could do was mutter, 'No . . .' in a weak, slurred voice.

A metallic tang caught in the back of her throat. Thick, undulating coils of *myst* spiralled out of the vortex and shot towards the mirrors, sinking into them, as though they were made out of water.

Darkness spread though the dreams, infecting and corrupting everything that it touched. Fast asleep, the children's smiles fell, to be replaced with blank, resigned expressions.

'It's working!' called out the Forefather, watching as wave upon wave of energy was fed back into the vortex from the mirrors. He raised the book high into the air and it almost seemed to purr in approval.

'Soon, we'll have enough power to convert the entire Dreamscape to our cause!' intoned the Forefather, his eyes blank and sightless. 'Ensuring the Umbra way continues. Forever, and always!'

'That is the Umbra way,' chanted the crowd, over and over.

'*That is the Umbra way.*'

CHAPTER 13

Faster and faster the *myst* spread. Before long there wasn't a single dream that wasn't infected. As the power from the dreams raced through the mirrors and into the hall, the vortex swirled and roared, like a raging fire.

Tiny hairs on Erika's neck rose up. The cool air crackled and buzzed, charged with intense power that kept on building and building. As the Forefather continued his chanting, the stones in the ceiling of the hall shifted around, slowly forming a huge opening, directly above the vortex. Another hole opened up in the room above that, and another

in the room above that, and *another* –
until soon, Erika could see a circle of
Dreamscape sky, far above her head.

'*SOON!*' roared the Forefather. 'Soon, our message will be delivered to the whole Dreamscape. Once Drythus and Despondia read the chosen words, the vortex will activate, transforming the tortured world above us into a sea of monotonous calm. Soon, there will only be Umbra!'

'*That is the Umbra way!*' chanted the crowd.

The Forefather turned and beckoned towards the tunnel behind him. Silas and his sister stepped out, walking in unison, both wearing long ceremonial robes. They were flanked by the Gloom forms of Wade and Beastling.

The Forefather held out the *Umbra Book of Sacred Texts* towards Silas and his sister.

With blank eyes, Despondia solemnly took hold of the book and then passed it to Silas. He took it silently and walked slowly towards the mouth of the vortex, stopping when he was almost next to Erika. He held the book open, ready to read from it.

The massive chamber was filled with noise. The assembled **Glooms** were still chanting and a relentless, whooshing, whining tone rose in pitch with each second, echoing out from deep within the vortex. So much was happening that nobody was paying any attention to Erika.

'Silas!' she gasped, struggling to get the words out. 'Silas, *listen* to me. You don't have to do this!'

His eyes flickered, the milky sheen drifted away and Silas struggled to look towards her.

'*I can't stop it!*' he hissed through gritted teeth. 'No matter how hard I try. The book is just too powerful.'

'That's not true!' insisted Erika, tears of frustration in her eyes. 'You don't have to do whatever that book tells you to! You can be whoever you want!' She looked at Silas's pained face.

'Come on, Silas!' she pleaded. 'This isn't you! It's the book. So, fight it! Come back to us! *Help us!*'

'I want to—' started Silas, then he jolted back and cried out in pain. 'But . . . not . . . *strong enough!*'

'You are!' insisted Erika. 'You just have to be *YOU*! Don't listen to that book, trying to tell you who you *should* be! It doesn't matter if you don't fit neatly into a tidy little box. *I* don't often fit in either. That's why *this* works!' She gestured between the two of them. 'You and me! Neither of us fit in where we're meant to, but our messy edges line up together perfectly. We fit well together because we don't fit in anywhere else! It's like Wade's grumpiness and Sim being so scatty.

We're *all* weird! And when we're together, none of us have to pretend that we're not! *Together*, we can do anything!'

'Yes—' began Silas but the book jerked violently in his hands and his eyes clouded over. Silas shook his head sharply, and his eyes returned to normal as he turned back to Erika.

'Fight it, Silas!' pleaded Erika. 'I *know* you can do this!'

As she looked at him, Silas's eyes flickered between the warm, friendly eyes that she recognized and the blank, empty eyes that belonged to a stranger.

Erika cried out as Silas stepped away from her, towards the vortex. A roaring cyclone of power tore through the chamber like a storm. Dust, grit and

debris shot through the air, biting into Erika's skin.

Lightning flashed and crackled around Silas, almost completely obscuring him. Tendrils of shadowy light licked out from the centre of the magical storm, rushing towards the ancient book in Silas's hands, as though the vortex could taste the power within it.

Erika could only watch as Silas slowly moved into the position that had been shown in the ancient pages of the book. He stood waiting for the final command. His head bowed. The roaring mass of energy in the room hummed and vibrated. Stones shook and Erika's vision blurred in and out of focus. The high-pitched keening sound from inside the vortex rose to an unbearable intensity.

'Now!' roared the Forefather. 'Speak the words of power!'

Erika watched as Silas braced himself against the tempest that tore through the air. Fingers tightly gripping the *Umbra Book of Sacred Texts*, he prepared to read the final command, which would convert the whole Dreamscape into sombre, joyless **Glooms**.

CHAPTER
14

Erika couldn't tear her eyes away from Silas. He buckled and twisted, teeth gritted, face contorted until eventually he screamed, 'No!'

With a sudden movement he hurled the ancient book right into the heart of the vortex. There was a moment's stillness, then the hall was in uproar. Everyone leaped to their feet, shouting. The Forefather wobbled unsteadily, his eyes perfect circles of horror.

'What have you done?' he gasped.

The vortex churned around where the book had been thrown into it. The power within it rose to a sudden, deafening crescendo and then in an explosion that threw Erika off her feet, it sent waves of energy bursting out in all directions. The thin, drifting shadow versions of Wade and Beastling flew towards the vortex as though caught up in a powerful current. With a splintering crash, all the ancient mirrors around the hall shattered and the *myst* within the dreams drifted down, dissolving harmlessly in the air as it went.

Within a minute it was all over. Silas fell to his knees, head bowed in front of the vortex. Erika dashed over to her friend and threw her arms around him.

'You did it, Silas!' she exclaimed. 'I *knew* you could!'

A troop of Gloom guards looked around, scratching their heads. They shifted their weapons uncertainly and stepped towards Silas, but Despondia ran over and stepped between them.

'If you want him, you'll have to come through me!' she warned, spinning a double-bladed sword through the air. The light glinted off the blade and she glared at the soldiers with narrowed eyes. The **Glooms** glanced at each other and then looked over towards the Forefather for instruction, but he just stood there, motionless, hands clasped to his face.

'Despondia?' whispered Silas. 'I don't understand. You'd stand against them, for *me*?'

'Well, you're my brother . . .' she replied quietly. 'When you left us before, it almost broke me, but Umbra aren't allowed to feel that way – so . . . I didn't let myself.' She paused, frowning and scratched the back of her neck.

'But now . . .' Again she paused and looked around. Then she started speaking with more confidence, 'Well, *now* I feel like I can say that out loud. I feel as though I can say lots of things I've kept hidden!'

'Er, yeah,' muttered the particularly gloomy-looking squadron leader. 'I know what you mean . . .' He looked sheepish. 'Sometimes I like to tell jokes. You know, in my chambers. On my own.'

All the other **Glooms** looked at him.

'You like to tell *jokes*?' asked the second in command, her mouth gaping open. The squadron leader flushed slightly, but then nodded insistently.

'Well, *yes*!' he blurted out. 'Yes, I do! And suddenly, I don't see what's so wrong with that!'

The second in command blinked in surprise and then whispered back quietly to the leader, '*Sometimes* I like to watch cat videos on the human people's internet.'

A strange sound came out of the

vortex – something between a drain gurgle and a burp – and Wade and Beastling stumbled out. They looked dazed, as though they had just woken up.

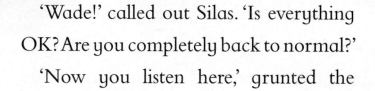

'Wade!' called out Silas. 'Is everything OK? Are you completely back to normal?'

'Now you listen here,' grunted the

thickset stone man, jabbing a finger at Silas's chest. 'You'd better not be expecting any thanks from me. After all, it was *you* that got us into this mess in the first place!'

'Looks like he's back to normal,' said Erika quietly.

Sim ran forwards, rubbing the side of her head. 'I have NO idea what just happened, and I've only just woken up, but it looks like somehow, someone saved the day!' She grabbed her friends and shouted, 'Group hug!'

Even though Wade groaned and pretended he was trying to wriggle out of it, Erika saw him patting Silas on the back when he didn't think anyone was watching.

After everything had settled down, the

Forefather rose to his feet. He looked around at the room.

'My family . . .' he said in a weak, trembling voice. 'Everything has changed. We no longer have the *Umbra Book of Sacred Texts*. We no longer have our mirrors into the humans' dreams. We have lost the details of all our rituals *and* our source of energy. From now on, we must make our own decisions about what we are going to do. It won't be easy though . . .' He broke off, and looked around, uncertain what to say next.

'No, it *won't* be easy!' called out Silas, stepping forward into the beam of moonlight that shone down from the sky far above their heads. 'It's never easy to make decisions about who you really are. But it's better than just blindly going along with everything that you are told to – especially if it makes you feel uncomfortable!'

'But how?' shouted someone from the back of the hall. 'How do we work out what to do next?'

'You just need to listen to the voice inside you!' said Despondia, stepping up beside her younger brother. 'Sometimes we try really hard to keep that voice quiet. I certainly did! It wasn't until I saw my brother being threatened that I realized he was more important to me than anything else. He's my brother! That's what the Umbra are. We're a family! But we were always too insular, too inward-looking. We were suspicious of everyone else, because we never *met* anyone else! But now –' she looked over at Erika and the rest of the **DREAM DEFENDERS** – 'I think that we can start trying to make some new friends. If . . . *if* you can forgive what we've done?'

She held out her hand to Erika, who

shook it warmly. Silas stepped closer and put his arm round his sister's shoulder and together they stood there, strong and determined. Somehow, Despondia seemed to grow taller. Everyone fell silent, waiting to see what she would say next.

'We can do this,' she said finally. 'This is a new chapter in the Umbra way, and from now on, we're going to write our own future. *Together!*'

CHAPTER 15

Erika stood in one of the upper chambers of the Umbra Citadel with the rest of the **DREAM DEFENDERS** and looked around. Now that light was beaming down from the huge opening in the ceiling above them, the whole place seemed a lot more welcoming. The grand carvings around each door looked beautiful and elegant rather than cold and austere. The whole Citadel seemed transformed, alive somehow, as though it had just woken up.

Erika was distracted by an Umbra boy

walking towards her. He was quivering with excitement.

'I've *always* wanted to do this!' he said, eyes gleaming. 'And *now* I am!'

'Do what?' asked Erika puzzled.

'Walk on the *right-hand* side of the corridor, of course!' explained the boy. 'It was always banned before, but now I can! What is it you humans say? "Yow-low"?'

'Sorry?' asked Erika.

Silas leaned in to whisper in her ear.

'You know, *Yow-low* . . . You only exist in this temporal stream for a limited and singular time.'

Erika grinned. '*YOLO! You Only Live Once!*' Erika smiled as the boy ran off down the right-hand side of corridor and then she turned to Silas. 'Looks like we're all wrapped up here then . . . You *are* coming back with us, aren't you?'

'Of course!' replied Silas. 'I couldn't leave you lot on your own with all your messy edges now, could I?'

Erika grinned at her friend. 'It's good to have you back,' she said and pulled him into a tight hug.

'Thank you,' whispered Silas. 'For everything.'

Despondia ran over to them. 'You'll

be coming back soon though, Drythus –
I mean, Silas – won't you?'

'Of course!' replied Silas.

'You can bring your friends too,' said
Despondia, looking at Erika, just as an
older Umbra lady rode
between them on a
unicycle, juggling
with fire.

'This is
amaaaaaaaazing!'
laughed the
lady as she
careered away
across the room.

'Thanks, Des,'
said Silas, hugging
his sister tight.

* * * * *

Sim, Beastling, Wade and Silas all walked Erika back to her dream portal.

'Well, here we are again . . .' said Erika. She bent down to give Beastling a hug. 'I'm so glad you're all back to normal!' she said ruffling his fur.

'**Heebie Jeebie!**' agreed Beastling, creating an image of two identical copies of himself.

'Er, two Beastlings?' guessed Erika.

Wade rolled his eyes. 'Me. Too!' he corrected. 'Seriously, Erika, you can do better than that!'

'Sorry, Beastling!' she said, but Beastling just nestled into her even more. Even though they no longer had the magical connection that had kept them literally stuck together, the bond of friendship between them was just as strong as ever.

'Thank you,' said Silas, looking at his friends. 'I *know* I should get kicked out of the **DREAM DEFENDERS** for what happened back there.'

'But it wasn't you,' said Erika, 'it was the book! Besides, in the end you did the right thing, and that's what matters.'

'So, we can all still be weirdos together?' asked Silas.

'I couldn't think of a better bunch of weirdos to hang out with,' replied Erika.

'Speak for yourself,' rumbled Wade, but he was smiling.

'Come on, Erika,' said Sim, peering at her watch. 'It's time for you to go!'

Erika waved at her friends as she stepped into her dream portal, and slowly began to fall awake.

CHAPTER 16

Beams of light slanted in through a crack in the curtains. Erika jumped out of bed and opened them fully, letting early morning sun wash over the room. She smiled as she stood there for a while. Another successful mission for the **DREAM DEFENDERS**. In fact, it had all been such an adventure, she could barely remember what had been happening in her daily life.

So, when Erika went downstairs and saw her parents sitting at the kitchen table with dark rings around their eyes, not speaking to each other, and a glum-looking Randall, she couldn't recall exactly what was going on.

Then she saw all the toys piled up around her brother and remembered what had happened yesterday. There was a Storm-Dogz action figure, a Speed-Wheels SKULL racer car with pull-back-and-go technology and a pirate hat. But Randall was ignoring them all.

'Oh, for *goodness*' sake!' exclaimed Erika, staring at her dad. 'What are you doing?'

'What?' said her dad looking flustered.

'These toys!' she continued. 'You know what he wants to play with. That doll from the cafe! Princess Sparkleadore – the one I have upstairs in my old toy box!'

'But Randall likes cars!' protested her dad.

'Sure he does!' said Erika. 'Cars are cool. But why does that mean he can't like dolls too?'

'I didn't say he couldn't!'

Erika looked at her dad, and slowly raised one eyebrow.

'Look, it's complicated!' said Erika's dad. 'You know, Randall's a boy . . . so he should, you know . . .'

'Oh, come off it, Dad!' interrupted Erika, her cheeks flushed. 'Randall is going to like the things that he likes and be the person that he's going to be. Just like I did. Just like *you* did! And if you try to force him to like what you *think* he should like, then it's not going to end well!'

There was silence in the kitchen, everyone was staring at her. Then Erika's dad turned to his wife and said, 'How did we end up with such a thoughtful, intelligent child?'

'I have *no* idea . . .' said Erika's mum with a small smile.

'Shall I get the doll then?' asked Erika. Her parents nodded and she ran upstairs.

It wasn't long before she had found Princess Sparkleadore, complete with glittery dress and amulet of power. '*Such a cool toy!*' muttered Erika, carrying the doll downstairs.

As soon as Randall saw what Erika was holding, his eyes lit up. He waved his arms around, reaching his hands out towards her.

'Here you go, buddy!' she said. 'And look, if you pull the cord on this one, she sings her song!'

With a smile that took over his whole face, Randall yanked the cord. Princess

Sparkleadore began to sing along to a retro-sounding power-pop song with synthesizers and electric guitars.

As the theme tune rang out, Erika's eyebrows shot up – her dad had started singing along with it.

'How come you know the words?' she asked.

'Well . . .' he said slowly. 'Princess Sparkleadore's a pretty old doll you know? We got her for you from a charity shop, but she was in a TV show back when *I* was a kid . . .' His cheeks flushed and he looked away. 'And you know what? I always kind of liked her, but my friends made me think I shouldn't be into things like that.' He paused, looking embarrassed. 'So, I pretended I didn't like her either. I bet you'd never be so silly?'

'Don't worry about it, Dad,' said Erika, punching him lightly on the arm. 'I'm sure that *one* day you might be as awesome as me.'

'Perhaps,' said her dad smiling, 'but I'm

sure I'll *never* be as modest.'

Erika grinned. All was well with the world. Her best friend was back to normal, her family were happy again and later that night she would have a brand-new, exciting adventure waiting for her in the Dreamscape.

All she had to do, was fall asleep.

Turn the page to read a sneak peek
from the first **DREAM DEFENDERS**
adventure *Erika and the Anger Mare*!

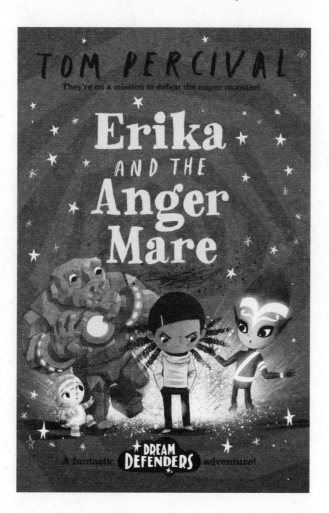

Erika Delgano was in a BAD mood.

Someone had chewed the fingers RIGHT OFF her favourite toy.

Someone had spilt blackcurrant juice ALL OVER her best T-shirt.

And *someone* had cried all the way through the school play, making her FORGET her lines.

This *someone* wasn't just anyone either.

They lived in her house, they had bewitched her parents and she couldn't get away from them, no matter what she did! This *someone* was her brother – Randall.

Admittedly Randall was only just over a year old and probably didn't mean to upset her, but all the same . . . With every day that passed, Erika grew crosser and crosser until she worried she might actually **POP!** Apparently nobody had ever *actually* popped from anger, but Erika was convinced that she would be the first.

Now, to cap it all off, she was stuck upstairs on yet another stupid TIME OUT while everyone else was downstairs, playing happy families.

Erika stomped around her room. When she was fed up with that, she kicked her bedpost. HARD. That hurt her foot, making her even crosser. So she picked up a bouncy ball and hurled it at the wall.

THUMP!

There! That *did* make her feel better (for about 0.3 seconds), until the ball bounced back and hit her on the nose.

DONK!

Erika wanted to cry. Randall had completely obliterated her picture. He'd even dribbled on it. But was *he* punished? Was *he* sent to his cot for a TIME OUT? *No he wasn't!*

Admittedly, she hadn't spent long on the picture, and she *had* left it on the floor, but still . . . it was *SO* unfair! Or at least that's how it seemed to Erika, but she was forgetting one rather important thing.

When Erika had seen the ruined picture, she'd run in and yelled at Randall, calling him '*A nasty little beast!*' and making him cry. That was the thing about Erika: when she lost her temper – she **REALLY** lost it.

And now here she was . . . Up in her

room with a bruised foot, a sore nose and an unpleasant squirming feeling in her tummy. If she hadn't been so angry, she might have realized that she felt a teeny bit bad about yelling at Randall – but she was still angry.

After a while, Erika heard her mum carrying Randall up to bed. She waited a couple of minutes and then tiptoed downstairs. She imagined having her dad all to herself; perhaps they'd have a game of football in the garden, like they used to . . . *before Randall.*

Erika found her dad in the kitchen. He was fast asleep at the table, his cheek cushioned on a half-eaten sandwich and his hand cradling a cold cup of tea. Drooling.

Erika shuddered – parents could be *really* disgusting sometimes.

'Dad?' she whispered.

No reply.

'Dad,' Erika repeated, more forcefully.

Still no reply.

DAD! she shouted in his ear.

'Whaaaa?' yelped Erika's dad, jerking upright and spilling cold tea down his shirt.

'Ah, you're awake,' said Erika innocently.

'Must have dropped off . . .' mumbled Erika's dad, rubbing his face and peeling a slice of cucumber off his cheek. He went to put it in his mouth, but stopped when he noticed Erika's expression. 'I'm just so tired at the moment . . .'

'Really?' interrupted Erika quickly. There was *nothing* worse than hearing your parents bore on about how tired they were, which her parents did.

ALL. THE. TIME.

Well, they did *now* . . .

'Anyway,' she continued, 'do you fancy a kick-about in the garden?'

'I'd love to . . .' said her dad, wiping a

dollop of
mustard from
his beard, 'but
I'd better get the
washing-up done.'

Erika's heart sank; he always *used* to
want to play football.

'What about *after* that?'

Erika's dad glanced up at the clock.

'I don't know . . .' he said. 'It's getting
late and Randall's been up a lot in the
night recently.'

'Mm-hmm,' mumbled
Erika. It was pretty
much her only
response whenever
her parents talked
about Randall.

'He gets terrible wind, you see,' added her dad.

'Mm–hmm,' muttered Erika.

'Of course, it might be a dairy intolerance . . .'

'Mm–hmm,' growled Erika.

'Either that or a—'

CARE!'

Erika exploded, surprising even herself.

'ALL YOU EVER DO IS TALK ABOUT RANDALL! YOU NEVER ASK ABOUT ME, YOU NEVER WANT TO SPEND TIME WITH ME!

IT'S ALL "RANDALL, RANDALL, RANDALL".'

She was shouting now.

'I WISH HE WASN'T EVEN HERE!'

For a few seconds she and her dad faced each other in the silent kitchen. There was a loud cry from upstairs then Erika's mum yelled down, '*Great!* You've woken Randall! That's just *perfect*. Thanks a lot.'

Hot tears prickled around Erika's eyes.

'Erika . . .' began her dad. 'I'm sorry. Listen, we can talk about—'

But Erika had gone. She'd pushed past her dad and run through the living room. Speeding upstairs, her feet beat out the rhythm of her thoughts.

IT'S *NOT* FAIR.

IT'S *NOT* FAIR.

IT'S *NOT* FAIR.

Erika barged inside her room and flung the door shut with a slam that shook the walls. She threw herself down on her bed, shoulders heaving with furious sobbing.

Eventually . . .
she fell asleep.

To be continued . . .

ACKNOWLEDGEMENTS

Seeing as this is book three in the 'Dream Defenders' series, I've already acknowledged a whole lot of people who have helped me to make these books, so the first thing that I would URGE you to do at this point is to pick up the first two books in the series and skip straight to the acknowledgements sections so that you can read the full list of who I feel I need to acknowledge. Go on, you pop off and do that now, I'll wait here . . .

There. Are you all up to speed? Good!

So, in addition to all those other people, I want to thank my agent Mandy Suhr for looking after my publishing schedules (and consequently my mental well-being!).

I also want to tip my hat to Marcus Rashford. Well, I would tip my hat if I were wearing one, but I don't like telling lies and I'm currently sitting on a train not wearing a hat at all. So, basically, I just wanted to flag up all the amazing work that Marcus does to help people who are having challenging times. From all his campaigning for free school meals to this incredible book club, he has made a real difference to thousands – if not millions – of children's lives. That's ON TOP of being a premier league and international footballer. Not a bad CV at all!

Finally, I just wanted to acknowledge creativity in general. Fifteen years ago I had an idea for a dark, fantasy adventure about a group of dream police who patrolled the borders between day and night. But I just couldn't get it to work. I tried making it a younger, middle-grade adventure story, but still it wasn't right. So I put it away and forgot about it. Then, many years later, when I was coming up with ideas for a new illustrated fiction series, the 'dream police' idea bubbled to the top of my mind. A few tweaks here, a few tweaks there (well, A LOT of tweaks actually) and suddenly an idea that I thought I'd never get to work has become a full series. It just goes to show how important it is to keep on trying, as you never know how anything in life is going to pan out.

And all I need to say now is HAPPY HALLOWEEN! Unless, of course, it's NOT Halloween when you read this, in which case you can put this book away now, pick it up again on 31st October and re-read this acknowledgements section.

And if you do that, THEN I'll tip my hat to you.

T.P.
August 2021

ABOUT THE AUTHOR

Tom Percival writes and illustrates all sorts of children's books. He has produced cover illustrations for the 'Skulduggery Pleasant' series, written and illustrated the 'Little Legends' series, the 'Dream Defenders' series, as well as twelve picture books. His 'Big Bright Feelings' picture book series includes the Kate Greenaway-nominated *Ruby's Worry*, as well as *Perfectly Norman* and *Ravi's Roar*. *The Invisible* is a powerful picture book exploring poverty and those who are overlooked in our society. In 2020 he created the animation Goodbye Rainclouds, for BBC Children in Need to celebrate unsung heroes and launch their campaign. He lives in Gloucestershire with his partner and their two children.

THE MARCUS RASHFORD BOOK CLUB

Look out for the Marcus Rashford Book Club logo – it's on books Marcus thinks you'll love!

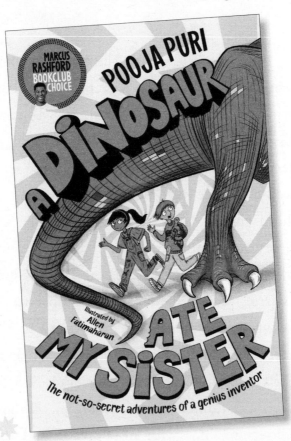

Marcus says: 'The perfect story to escape into and find adventure. Pooja is super talented and I'm a big fan!'

Marcus says: 'Fun, engaging, action-packed — I would have loved this book as a child!'

THE MARCUS RASHFORD
BOOK CLUB

The Marcus Rashford Book Club is a partnership between Marcus Rashford MBE and Macmillan Children's Books (MCB) that aims to help you find books that Marcus thinks you'll love! Look out for the Marcus Rashford Book Club logo to find the books that Marcus recommends.

Two books will be chosen each year by Marcus and the MCB team, to make sure that children all over the country can own their very own book – reading is for everyone, no matter who you are or where you come from. The book club will feature an exciting selection of titles, to make sure that everyone finds something just right for them.

The book club launched in June 2021, with the laugh-out-loud, time-travel adventure, *A Dinosaur Ate My Sister* by Pooja Puri, illustrated by Allen Fatimaharan. The next book, launching in October 2021, is *Silas and the Marvellous Misfits* by Tom Percival, an action-packed adventure that will show you how to banish your worries. These books will be available in shops, and to make sure that all children have access to them, free copies will also be given out to support under-privileged and vulnerable children across the UK.

magic breakfast
fuel for learning

You know what happens when a car runs out of fuel or battery power don't you, it just stops! Well, it's pretty much the same for people. When we don't have enough food or drink inside us, we don't have the energy we need to be able to do all the things we want and need to do in a day.

Magic Breakfast is a charity that works with lots of schools in England and Scotland to help them make sure all their pupils eat a healthy breakfast, so they are full of energy for the morning ahead.

Magic Breakfast is pleased to have joined Marcus Rashford and Macmillan Children's Books to ensure thousands of children from its partner schools receive books from Marcus Rashford's Book Club. Together we aim to encourage reading for pleasure amongst children, especially those who may not have their own books at home.

www.magicbreakfast.com

Being able to read, write, speak and listen well can change someone's life: these skills don't just help throughout school and work, they also support overall well-being. Books and reading are a brilliant way to boost these important literacy skills but unfortunately, the National Literacy Trust research shows 380,000 children don't own a single book of their own. The charity is a proud partner of Marcus Rashford's Book Club to help provide children and young people with access to books and their life-changing benefits.

It's the National Literacy Trust's mission to improve the literacy levels of those who need support most. It runs Literacy Hubs and campaigns with schools and families in communities where low literacy seriously impact people's life chances. The charity has a huge range of literacy-building resources and activities online for children and young people of all ages, including complementary resources for this brilliant new Book Club.

www.literacytrust.org.uk

BT have brought together Hope United, a team of the very best footballers who want to make the internet a safer and friendlier space for everyone. Along with players such as Marcus Rashford, Andy Robertson, Jordan Henderson, Trent Alexander-Arnold and Lucy Bronze, Hope United want to get rid of hate and bullying, and to show us all how being online can be more hopeful.

BT works hard to connect people across the world, and to make exciting ideas come to life. We're always developing new ways for you to talk to your family and friends, wherever they may be.

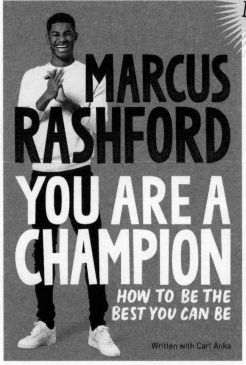

MARCUS RASHFORD

YOU ARE A CHAMPION

HOW TO BE THE BEST YOU CAN BE

Written with Carl Anka

'I want to show you how you can be a champion in almost anything you put your mind to.'

Marcus Rashford MBE is famous worldwide for his skills both on and off the pitch – but before he was a Manchester United and England footballer, and long before he started his inspiring campaign to end child food poverty, he was just an average kid from Wythenshawe, South Manchester. Now the nation's favourite footballer wants to show YOU how to achieve your dreams, in this positive and inspiring guide for life.